Kids' Secret Playbook of Life

SHORT, FUNNY LIFE STORIES FOR KIDS 8-12.
TEACHES FRIENDSHIPS AND SOCIAL SKILLS

Panama Pete

This book is dedicated to kids to help them grow up.

Contents

Chapter 1

Introduction

> *"The older you* get, *the better you get. Unless you're a banana."*

Now that you have your very own **Kid's Secret Playbook of Life** book, your life will be easier. Here's why.

This secret playbook has the answers to lots of questions and many situations you're dealing with in life.

In the stories in the following chapters, I'll reveal how I've handled many of these life situations and what I learned along the way. Many of the stories are funny or talk about funny situations.

A lot of situations are funny when you look back at them and many things are funny when they're happening to somebody else. But some situations are not funny—especially when they're happening to you. We'll talk about those situations too.

Let's get started

If you've read my previous book, **_Confidence and Life Skills for Kids Ages 8–12_**, you already know all about me, but in case you haven't read that book, let me introduce myself.

Hello. My name is Peter, but my parents call me Pete.

Everyone at school calls me Panama Pete because I used to live in Panama. My parents moved to Panama a few years ago, and we lived there for two years. Now we're back in the US.

The kids at school started calling me Panama Pete. At first, I didn't like it because I thought they were making fun of me.

But then I decided I liked it. It made me special. No one else at the school had ever lived in a different country. I doubt that many of them had ever even visited a foreign country.

More about me

I started middle school this year. I'm finding it to be harder, but more fun than middle school.

I have an older sister named Becky and a younger brother named Noah.

That's enough about my family. Let me tell you about my dog. I won't say that he's just like one of the family because every time I hear someone say that their dog is just like one of the family, I want to ask them, "Which one?"

My dog's name is Perro. Perro is the Spanish word for dog. That would be a funny name for a dog in Panama. It would be like giving a dog in the US the name "Dog."

Perro is a medium size black dog with short hair. He has one ear that flops down, but other than that, he's just an ordinary-looking dog.

We got him as a rescue dog from an animal shelter soon after we moved back to the US, and I named him Perro to remind me of Panama because everybody there speaks Spanish.

When I tell someone that my dog's name is Perro, I don't think many people realize his name means dog in Spanish. If they do, no one has ever said so.

He belongs to the whole family, but I spend the most time with him and he acts like he's my dog.

His bed is in my room, and I take him out in the mornings, and I'm the one who feeds him.

He always wants to go outside first thing every morning. When he comes back in, he always rushes over to his bowl to see what's in it. I don't know why he's in such a hurry to see what's in his bowl. It's always the same thing—one cup of dry dog food.

We don't feed him anything from the table, but he still begs sometimes. You would think he would learn not to beg since he never gets anything, but he still does it.

That's enough right now about me, my family, and my dog. I'll tell you more as we go along.

At the end of each chapter, I include a section called "**Takeaway**" to remind you of the most important things I discussed in that chapter. That way, it will be easier for you to remember what we've just talked about and what you can take away from what you just learned.

I also include a "**Try This**" section at the end of each chapter to show you how you can use the information you learned from the chapter in your life. Sometimes this section will include something to do and sometimes it will be something for you to think about.

The Takeaway

The interesting thing to remember or take away from this chapter is that now you have your own playbook of life that will show you how to deal with many of the problems and situations you encounter in school and in life.

Another thing to remember or take away from this chapter is that, just like there are things in school you have to learn, there are things in life you need to learn as well. This *Secret Playbook of Life* book will help you learn how to handle situations before they arrive. Life's events will not catch you off guard.

Try This

The next time you have a problem in your life, stop and think, *Will this even matter a week from now?* (Probably not.) If it won't matter a week from now, why let it bother you now? Doing this will prevent a lot of situations in your life from ever being a problem.

Chapter 2

Fit in or Stand Out?

> *"All you need is love. But a little chocolate now and then doesn't hurt."*

We all want to fit in, but we also want to stand out, be noticed, and be special.

You don't have to be one or the other. The good news is that it's possible to fit in and stand out at the same time.

When I moved back to the US after living in Panama for two years, I was eager to fit in. But when kids started calling me Panama Pete, that made me stand out, but I wasn't sure it helped me fit in.

At first, I didn't like being called Panama Pete because I thought the other kids were making fun of me. Then I decided I liked it because it made me stand out.

I could speak Spanish and English and nobody else in the school could speak Spanish. Even the Spanish teacher wasn't very good at it. She was always asking me how to say something in Spanish.

The kids who were taking her Spanish class were learning a few words and some verbs. They were learning to read some Spanish, but they were not learning to speak much Spanish.

Being the only kid in school who had lived in a different country was another thing that made me special.

I had the "standing out" thing covered. I was different, and everyone noticed me, but now I had to find a way to fit in.

Some kids have the opposite problem, or at least they think they do. They fit in so well that they don't think they stand out. They don't think they're special in any way.

You really can fit in and stand out at the same time

Sometimes I see kids trying too hard to fit in.

You might feel that the more special you are, the less you'll be able to fit in. But that's not true.

The best way to fit in is to be yourself and not try too hard.

I've seen kids intentionally not score well on tests. They think if their grade is too high, they'll be called a nerd and that will keep them from fitting in.

Other times, I've seen kids do dangerous things or things they know they shouldn't do, hoping to be special.

It's natural to want to fit in and be one of the group, but there are some groups you don't want to fit in with or be a part of. Always keep this in mind.

The two best ways to fit in

I've found that one way to fit in is to just be myself.

If you show a genuine interest in other kids, that will help you fit in more than anything else. Listen to them when they're talking, and to show that you're really listening, comment or ask them a question about something they've said.

All kids want to be around kids who will listen to them, understand them, and think what they're saying is important and worth listening to.

The second way I've found to fit in is to try to always be happy and positive. That's not easy to do, but try to look on the bright side of every situation, even when things are not going the way you want them to.

Don't be negative, constantly complaining, or unhappy. Try to be happy as much as possible.

I like to be around happy and positive kids and other kids do too. Maybe that's why I have fun playing with my new neighbor, Lily. She's almost always in a good mood. I'll tell you more about her in the next chapter.

You really can fit in and stand out at the same time.

The Takeaway

Being different is a good thing. Whether you're overweight, short, don't think you're pretty, or just generally feel different and out of place, don't worry about these things. They're not as important as you think.

As Kermit the Frog said, "It's not easy being green."

Sometimes it seems like it's not easy being a kid either.

Be yourself, be happy, and be positive, and you'll fit in.

Try This

Don't try too hard to fit in. Be yourself, show genuine interest in other kids, listen to them, and comment when they talk (this shows that you actually listened and that you're interested in what they said).

Chapter 3

My New Neighbor

> *"I remember it as if it were yesterday. Of course, I don't really remember yesterday all that well."*

Over the summer, my best friend Billy's family, who lived across the street from me, sold their house and moved away.

I thought my summer would be boring without Billy. I wouldn't have anybody to play with or hang out with.

Then, about a week later, a new family moved into Billy's house. They have one kid, a girl named Lily. She is a year younger than Billy and me, but she's older than my little brother.

She's a lot of fun. She doesn't have bad hair days like my older sister, Becky, and she enjoys playing outside. Yesterday, I showed her how to fly a kite. We had a lot of fun and my kite didn't get caught in a tree this time.

Last Saturday, Lily went fishing with me in Mr. Taylor's pond, which is near my house. Billy and I used to go fishing there. Mr. Taylor lets me go fishing in his pond and I usually catch a few fish, but Lily and I didn't catch anything. We got some nibbles and we had a lot of fun.

Lily wasn't a sissy. She put a worm on her own hook. Becky won't do that. I have to bait her hook when we go fishing, but we don't go often because she doesn't like to fish. She doesn't like to do many of the things that I think are fun.

Becky doesn't play with me much like she used to do. She has a boyfriend now and she spends a lot of time on the phone talking to him.

Lily is different—she's fun to be around. She's not usually grumpy, and she doesn't have many bad hair days where nothing pleases her, like Becky does. Maybe that will change when she gets older, but I hope not.

She reminds me of Perro in a lot of ways because she's always happy and never complains. But I better not tell her she reminds me of my dog. I don't think she would enjoy being compared to a dog.

Lily doesn't have a dog, but she loves to play with Perro and he loves getting more attention and having another person to play with.

Lily said she used to be afraid of dogs, but after spending time with Perro and playing with him, she's trying to convince her parents to let her get a dog.

My little brother, Noah, and my new friend, Lily, look up to me and are constantly asking me questions. They seem to think I know everything.

I was convinced that I would have a boring summer when Billy moved away. But Lily and I had fun all summer and Noah played with us sometimes. It's hard to believe that the summer is gone and school has started again.

The Takeaway

If you think something won't be any fun, keep an open mind and see how it turns out. It could surprise you. I realized that my most enjoyable summer I've ever had was this one and I had thought it was going to be boring.

Try This

Think of something that's coming up in your life that you think will not be any fun. Now imagine all the things that could happen that would turn it into one of the most enjoyable times of your life. After you think of some of those things, maybe there's something you could do to help make them happen. If not, keep an open mind and see what happens. Maybe something that you didn't even imagine ends up happening and the thing you thought was going to be boring will be super fun.

Chapter 4

Riding a Horse

"Whoever said money can't buy happiness simply didn't know where to go shopping."

I went to summer camp again this summer. I went last year, and that's when I learned how to swim.

This year, I went to a different summer camp. I don't know which camp I liked better. We did different things.

The most enjoyable thing we did differently at this camp was that we rode horses a lot. At least, it was enjoyable after I learned how to stay on a horse and not fall off.

On the first day, they asked who could ride a horse. About half the kids raised their hands. I wanted to fit in, so I raised my hand too. I had never ridden a horse, but they didn't ask who had ever ridden a horse before.

I wasn't being untruthful because they didn't ask who had ridden a horse. They just asked who could ride a horse, and since I was sure that I could, I raised my hand.

They sent the kids who had never ridden a horse over to the corral. They placed them on a horse and led the horse around in circles inside the corral. That didn't look like any fun at all, at least not compared to getting on a horse and riding along a trail. That's what the kids who knew how to ride (or said they could ride) did.

On the first day, I watched the other kids getting on their horses. I noticed that they all got on from the left side. I didn't know why, but I did the same thing and got on my horse from the left side.

When I first got on my horse, I felt like I should have a seatbelt to keep from falling off. We took off down the trail. There were five of us, and my horse was the third horse in the line.

My horse was only walking, but I thought my heart was going to gallop right out of my chest, I was so excited.

In the beginning, staying on my horse took my full concentration, but after a little while, I felt like I had mastered the art of not falling off. The longer we rode, the more natural staying on my horse felt. Pretty soon, there was nothing to it. It just felt natural. I was enjoying riding a horse.

Then the lead horse started going a little faster, and all the other horses went faster to keep up. That's when the trail made a sharp turn to the right and went up a hill.

When my horse made that sharp turn and started up the hill, that's when I fell off. I guess I wasn't paying enough attention. I hit the ground hard and rolled down the hill. My horse stopped, and all the other horses stopped.

I wasn't seriously hurt, but my ego took a major hit.

When I finally stood up, everybody was looking at me and laughing. I thought, *I wish I had rolled all the way down the hill where nobody could see me.*

I finally got back up the hill and got on my horse. Throughout the rest of the day, every time we would come to a sharp turn or start up a hill, somebody would say, "Hold on, Panama Pete." They were all having fun at my expense.

Maybe in the beginning I should have said that I didn't know how to ride a horse, but if I had done that, I would probably still be sitting on a horse in the corral going around in circles with somebody leading my horse. That doesn't sound like nearly as much fun as I was having. Even though I fell off of my horse and everyone laughed at me, I still had a great time.

Falling off a horse was not the end of the world. It actually made the day more interesting.

The Takeaway

Accept the fact that unexpected things are going to happen in life. Sometimes you'll make a mistake, and people will laugh at you. Look on the bright side. At least you made everybody else's day more enjoyable.

Learn to laugh at yourself and at your mistakes. Life is more fun that way.

Try This

The next time you make a mistake and people laugh at you, instead of feeling embarrassed, laugh too and enjoy the event.

Keep in mind that it's not the mistake people will remember—it's what you did after the mistake. It's how you recovered.

Chapter 5

Grandpa's Farm

> *"Trust yourself. You know more than you think you do."*

The most fun I had this summer was when I spent two weeks staying with Grandma and Grandpa on their farm.

Every morning, Grandpa and I would go to the barn and feed the cows, and then later, we would go back and let them out to spend the day in the pasture eating grass.

About mid-morning, I would go with Grandma and we would feed her chickens and gather the eggs.

They had a routine and they did the same thing every morning—even on Saturdays and Sundays.

One of the most exciting things I did was when Grandpa let me drive his tractor. He had an old red Farmall Cub tractor. It was an antique. I checked Google and found that they stopped making that model tractor in 1979, so it really was an antique.

He said he had bought it used several years ago. He always kept it in the barn and in good condition.

It was a small tractor—way bigger than a riding lawnmower but still smaller than most tractors.

The first time he let me drive, it was out in the cow pasture. I had the whole cow pasture, so I wasn't likely to run over anything. I was sure I could drive it.

Grandpa showed me how to use the clutch and change gears. It looked like there was nothing to it. But the first time I put it in gear and let out on the clutch, the tractor leaped forward and the engine died. Grandpa had told me to let out on the clutch slowly, but obviously, I didn't do it slowly enough.

It took me two more tries before I was able to get the tractor going. Steering after I got it going was not any problem at all, but it took me two days of driving the tractor around in the cow pasture before I could get it going and change the gears to go faster without making the tractor jerk.

After a few afternoons driving the tractor around the pasture, I felt like I had learned how to drive the tractor, and there was nothing to it. Grandpa thought I was doing a good job, too. He said he thought I was driving well enough that I could drive the tractor into the barn and park it for the night. Until now, he had always been doing that.

I was excited to get to put the tractor in the barn and I knew I could do it. Since there was plenty of room on each side to get the tractor into the barn, I knew I wouldn't have to be perfect.

I was going slowly and watching each side as I pulled the tractor into the barn. I was feeling proud of myself, and then, boom—I ran the tractor into the back of the barn. This happened because I was busy watching both sides and forgot to watch the front.

It didn't hurt the tractor, but it knocked two boards loose on the back of the barn. Thankfully, Grandpa could nail them back.

The Takeaway

It's good to have confidence in yourself and believe that you can do almost anything, such as ride a horse, drive a tractor, or learn a new skill. But be careful because sometimes you may have more confidence than skill and you may believe that you can do things better than you really can.

It happened to me when riding a horse and when driving a tractor. The good news is that in both cases, I learned how to do something new and I had fun.

Try This

The next time you're thinking about doing something you've never done before, say to yourself, "I think I can do this, but it may take me some practice and I may have to learn how. I may not do it right the first time, but I'm going to give it my best effort and learn as I go."

Chapter 6

Making Friends

"When I was a kid, my parents moved a lot, but I always found them."

When Lily moved in across the street from me this summer, it wasn't long before I wanted to be her friend.

When I first thought about why I wanted to be her friend, I was confused. She was younger than I was and I like friends my age, or maybe even a year or two older. What was it about Lily that made me want to be her friend?

When I thought about it more, here's what I came up with:

- Lily was almost always happy.

- She didn't complained much and few things seemed to upset her.

- She was interested in me and what I was doing.

- She was always asking me my opinion and what I thought about things.

- She listened to what I said and often asked questions about things I had said. That showed me she actually listened to what I had said.

I decided if those were the things that made me want to be Lily's friend, maybe I should do the same things she does and people would want to be my friend.

The next day, I stopped complaining. (Well, I didn't completely stop complaining. I still complained a little, but not nearly as much as I had been doing.) There were still plenty of things that bothered me and things I was unhappy with sometimes, but I tried not to say anything to anybody about them.

After all, complaining and being unhappy did no good and never changed anything.

I started showing interest in other people, what they were doing and what they thought. I wasn't just faking it because I was genuinely interested in them. The more I got to know them the more interested I became in them, what they were doing and what they were interested in.

Pay people a compliment or ask them a question

Below are examples of comments you can say. Not all the comments and questions below will fit every situation, but use them when they fit.

- I liked the comment you made in class today.

- What you just said is interesting.

- I like your shirt.

- I agree with what you said.

- What do you think about (whatever)? Asking people what they think about something shows that you value their opinions.

Once, my grandpa told me that asking people a question that would allow them to talk about themselves is a good idea.

Then, since he's always full of humor, he said, Grandma is always asking me, *"What in the world is wrong with you?"* He said, *"Even though that question encourages me to talk about myself, I don't think it's a good example of a question to ask someone."*

Here are the two things that worked the best to help me make more friends

#1. Don't be negative. Try to always be happy. No one likes to be around negative people. Don't complain about anything regardless of how bad you think a situation is. (The fact that she didn't complain much and was almost always happy was one of the main things that made me want to be friends with Lily.)

#2. Be genuinely interested in other kids. Pay them compliments and ask them questions about themselves. Don't talk about yourself, what you're doing or have done unless they ask. They're not interested in you until they get to know you.

There's an old saying that says, "People don't care how much you know until they know how much you care."

The Takeaway

To make friends, don't be negative or complain. Be happy. Show genuine interest in the person you want to be friends with. Don't talk about yourself. When you're talking with someone, don't interrupt them. Let them talk and then ask a question about what they said. This shows that you were listening.

Try This

First, stop complaining and being negative. Smile and be happy. Then think about someone you would like to be friends with. Have a question ready you can ask them. Compliment them on something about themselves or something they said or did recently. Then let the conversation go from there.

Chapter 7

Trying Different Things

> *"I'm not stupid. My mother had me tested."*

Some kids in my class, and even several adults I know, never want to do anything different or even eat anything different.

Doing things differently reminds me of Helen Keller, a famous author who lost her hearing and sight before she was two years old. I've been reading about her. She learned to speak and accomplish a lot of things even though she was blind and couldn't hear.

She said, *"Life is either a daring adventure or nothing at all."*

I think her whole life was an adventure. She certainly did a lot of things differently.

I'm convinced that if you do the same things all the time, you'll have no adventures in your life.

If I never did anything different or took any chances—maybe I would be safer and I wouldn't get hurt or embarrassed, but that would be a boring way to live.

I also like to try different foods. When they serve something different for lunch at school, some of the kids won't even try it.

I'm always eager to try new foods. Sometimes (maybe a lot of times) I end up biting into something I don't like, but sometimes I find something that's really delicious. To me, trying different foods is at least worth taking one bite. How bad could one bite be?

The same goes for doing different things

A lot of kids are afraid to do something they've never done before.

I remember being scared on my first day at a new school and I remember feeling scared the first time I got on a horse.

I didn't have a choice about starting the new school, but I could have decided not to get on the horse.

It amazes me how many kids choose not to do something they've never done before. There's no adventure if they do that.

It would be like not getting in the swimming pool until you have learned how to swim. I've found that when I overcome my fear and do things I've never done before, that's when the adventure starts and that's when I have the most fun.

I know the feeling. Whether I'm making a speech, acting in a school play, learning to swim, or riding a horse for the first time, I always feel scared to start with.

When I was learning to swim at camp last summer, the instructor scared me when he told me to put my face in the water. I couldn't breathe and it was scary. Even though I was standing on the bottom of the pool and I could raise my head anytime, it was still scary.

The Takeaway

Fear is a way of keeping us safe and many times it's a good idea not to do things you're afraid to do. When fear tells you not to jump off of a building or not to step out into traffic, pay attention to that fear and don't do those things.

But if there's no real chance you will get hurt if you do something you're afraid to do, that's when you should do it and enjoy the adventure.

Try This

Think of a time when you were afraid to do something, but after you did it you were glad you did. I bet you can think of several times when you did something you were afraid to do, but after you did it you were glad that you did.

Chapter 8

Major Upsets

"You can kid the world, but not your older sister."

What I call a major upset is when something totally unexpected changes your world and there's nothing you can do about it.

Your only option is to live with the situation, regardless of how hopeless it seems.

You go along worrying about a history test that's coming up, math homework you haven't finished, and a rained-out soccer game. You consider all these things as problems, but then, wham. Out of the blue, a major, real problem that's truly upsetting hits you.

Unfortunately, these upsetting events happen in life and they can totally change your world, but you can survive. It takes a firm determination to get through these major upsetting events, but if you're strong and determined, you can do it. And I believe that describes you, or you wouldn't be reading this book.

Here are some major upsets I've experienced—and survived

- **When my parents told me we were moving to Panama.** I didn't even know where it was. I couldn't find it on the world map I had in my room.

- **When we came back to the US after living for two years in Panama, life was just as terrifying.** We didn't move back to the same town—not even back to the same state. Everything was just as foreign to me as when we moved to Panama.

- **The day the doctor told me I was allergic to peanuts.** I'm not just a little allergic. If I eat something with a tiny amount of peanuts or something that was cooked in peanut oil, it could be deadly for me. So, it's not that I just could no longer eat peanut butter. Peanuts are in some store-bought cookies and many store-bought items that don't have peanuts warn that they could have cross-contamination because the factory uses peanuts to make other items. Many people cook food in peanut oil. Worst of all, when I'm at a birthday party or a friend's house, I can't eat most things because I never know if they contain peanuts.

- **The day I started at a new school.** I think starting at a new school was the scariest thing of all.

I'm sure there will be more major upsets in my life that I can't do anything about. And I know that when major upsets happen in my life, complaining, getting mad, or feeling and acting sad won't fix or change anything.

I just have to deal with the situation and life goes on. Life's different, but it goes on.

The only good thing is that after living through some of these major upsets, I'm convinced that it's not the end of the world, even though it feels like it sometimes. Best of all, I know I can survive anything the world throws at me.

The Takeaway

Realize that besides minor everyday problems, major upsets are going to happen in your life. And to survive these major upsets, or life-changing events, you have to take the attitude that you can handle anything the world throws at you. That's easier said than done, but you can do it.

Try This

Think of a situation in your life where you thought life was unfair. Something happened that you had no control over and there was nothing you could do to change anything. That's what I would call a major upset. Maybe you thought your life, as you knew it, was over.

When you think back on one of these situations, stop and realize that you survived and found a way to handle it.

Also realize that you're strong and you can handle anything else the world throws at you. It won't always be easy, but you can do it.

Chapter 9

Some Days Are Just Bad

> *"It ain't what you don't know that gets you into trouble. It's what you know for sure that just ain't so."* said famous writer, Mark Twain.

Some days are bad from the very beginning.

I have bad days sometimes, but not often. My sister, Becky, has a lot of bad days. I sometimes think she has more bad days than good days.

On days when she's having a bad hair day, it seems like she doesn't like anything in the universe, including me. She doesn't always act like I'm her biggest problem, but some days I'm convinced that she thinks I am.

Some days she plays with me and we have fun. The other day, she even asked me what I thought about something, like my opinion mattered to her. That was a first.

I don't think my friend Lily has many bad days. I'm sure she has some, but I don't remember hearing her complain even a little. She is usually happy. Maybe that's why everybody wants to be her friend.

I'm learning more all the time that kids don't want to be around kids who are always complaining.

When I got home today, my grandpa was there. He had stopped by to visit. I always enjoy talking to him. He has a lot of good information, but he never lectures me. He usually gets his point across just by asking me a question.

I was complaining about how bad my day had been. I told him I was trying not to complain so much, but some days are so bad I feel I have to.

He said, "How is that working out for you?" He was right. Complaining didn't make my day any better.

Back to my bad day

Today was so bad that I needed to complain—at least to myself, if not to anyone else. Let me tell you about my day.

Some problems with my day were my fault, but not all of them.

Last night, I watched a movie on TV with my family instead of finishing my math homework. It would not be a problem, I thought, because I could get up early and finish my homework before I caught the bus.

But that didn't happen. Instead of getting up early, I overslept. Mrs. Baker doesn't always take up math homework, but with my luck, she did today.

The weather forecast said it was going to rain all day, so we wouldn't have soccer practice today. My best friend, Billy, called me last night, and said he was sick and wouldn't be at school today. When I got to school, I remembered that school pictures were going to be taken today and I had worn the worst shirt I own.

Look for the good things that happened on bad days

At first, I couldn't think of anything that was good about today.

But if I changed my attitude and tried harder, maybe there were a few good things about today. After some thought, here's a new view of my day.

- Missing a day of soccer practice wasn't all bad. I had more time to spend talking to my friends.

- Billy wasn't there, but I ended up sitting with some new friends at lunch. That worked out well.

- The shirt I was wearing in the school pictures was an old shirt, but it was my favorite shirt, so I'm happy with the pictures.

The Takeaway

Even what looks like a bad day won't seem as bad as you thought if you stop and try to find some good things about the day.

If you tell your brain that it's going to be a bad day, your brain will find bad things about the day and prove you right, but if you tell your brain the day is going to be good, it will find some good things about your day. That's how your brain works.

Try This

The next time you're having a bad day, stop and look for the good things about the day. Think about the last time you had a bad day. I'm sure there were some things about the day that you didn't like. But try hard and see if you can't find a few good things about what you thought was a bad day.

Also, when you think about the things that made the day bad, did any of those things matter a week later?

Chapter 10

Bullies

> *"Bullying has nothing to do with you. It's the bully who is insecure."*

I've seen a lot of kids being bullied at school. I don't know what makes some kids want to be bullies, but it seems there are always some around.

I think most bullies don't fit in, so they try to stand out and get attention by being bullies. Maybe that's not true, but that's my opinion.

Bullies want to get attention, to be seen as being in control, and to feel powerful. They don't want to be ignored.

But most bullies are insecure and have lots of fears.

Here's what bullies are afraid of:

Being ignored. They want attention.

Public humiliation. They don't want to be shamed or lose their power or authority in front of their peers.

Being exposed. They are terrified that they will look weak.

Bullies target a lot of kids. You might experience bullying. Don't worry about it. You can handle the bully and put him in his place. I'll show you how to deal with a bully.

How I deal with a bully

I was being bullied all the time in school this year. Tom was a little bigger than I was and he was always picking on me. To put it nicely, he was a royal pain.

He would pull my ear in class when the teacher wasn't looking. He would bump into me hard in the hall and then say in a very insincere way, "I'm sorry." And he would sometimes knock my drink over in the cafeteria or spill things on me.

We had a substitute teacher one day and Tom was being especially irritating. I told the teacher about it after the class and she told me to try ignoring him. She said bullies want attention and want to irritate you. If you ignore them and they don't get a reaction out of you, their behavior is not any fun for them and they'll likely stop bullying you and try bullying somebody else.

I had tried ignoring him and that seemed to work for a little while. But then he started bullying me again.

When I told my grandpa about the bullying, he told me what he did one time when he was being bullied in school. He said, "Try embarrassing him."

He told me the words to say to do that. So the next time Tom pulled my ear, here's what I said to him loud enough for everyone to hear.

I said, "Tom, are you in love with me? My grandma loves me dearly and she doesn't put her hands on me nearly as much as you do."

Everybody laughed at him and he didn't bother me again.

Four ways to deal with a bully

- **Ignore them.** Try this first. This usually works. Bullies want attention and they want a reaction out of you. When they don't get a reaction out of you, it's no fun for them.

- **Embarrass them.** Give it some thought and find ways to embarrass them when other kids are around. This technique almost always works.

- **Be firm and assertive with them and tell them to stop immediately.** If you show the bully that you're serious, and it's not a game, many times they'll stop their bullying.

- **Report them to an authority.** Finally, if the previous three actions don't stop the bullying, report the bully and his actions to a teacher or counselor. And if the bullying still doesn't stop, report the situation to a higher authority such as the principal or law enforcement if necessary. You don't have to put up with bullying.

You have the power to make the bully stop, so do whatever is necessary to make it stop. You don't have to put up with their behavior—ever.

The Takeaway

A bully just wants to get a reaction out of you.

When you show him that what he's doing bothers you, that gives him what he wants and he'll do the same thing over and over.

Try This

First, when you're being bullied, just ignore the bully. Don't show any reaction. Act as if he doesn't exist.

If ignoring the bully doesn't work, embarrass him and make him look small.

If those two techniques don't work, report him and his actions to an authority. You don't have to put up with being bullied.

> **Note:** Anytime you feel threatened or think the bully might hurt you, don't put up with that for a minute. Immediately report him and his actions to a teacher, your parents, or an adult with authority.

Chapter 11

Comparing Myself to Others

> *"My sister said I don't listen to her—at least, I think that's what she said."*

When I compare myself to others, it's obvious that I'm a big failure. At least, that's the way I see it.

I hear kids all the time talking about all the amazing things they've accomplished—making a 100 on a test, winning a track meet, girls making the cheerleading squad, etc.

I see all the photos posted on social media of other kids having fun and doing fun things. It always looks like everything in their lives is perfect.

They talk about their accomplishments and I haven't done any of those things.

For accomplishments, I feel like it's a major accomplishment if I can get my leg through my underwear in the mornings without falling.

I was talking to my grandpa about what a failure I was.

He said when he thinks about comparing himself to others, it reminds him of the time he was sitting on a park bench and two old men were sitting on a bench nearby. One man asked the other, "How's your wife?" The other man said, "Compared to what?"

What are you really comparing yourself to?

When you're comparing yourself to other people, it's important to remember that most likely you're not seeing the real other person. You're seeing the edited version they want you to see. It's the version they wish were real.

When you look at all those perfect pictures, remember that they probably took a dozen or more photos to get just the right one, and even then, they most likely tweaked the photo with Photoshop before posting it.

As my grandpa said, "Compared to what?" Don't compare yourself to someone else's imagination of what they wish was the real them.

Sometimes I think I'm dumb as an ox. I don't know if an ox is dumb or not. I've never even seen an ox, but I've heard the phrase, "dumb as an ox," all my life, so maybe they are dumb.

Maybe I'm dumb too.

Some kids seem to always have the right answers in class. They're the first to raise their hands and they always have their homework completed.

A lot of time in class, I don't know the right answer, and when I think I do sometimes, I'm wrong.

I'm not the smartest kid in the class and, as they say, I'm not the brightest light on the string or the sharpest knife in the drawer. I know I could study harder and spend more time doing my homework. My goal when I'm doing my homework is to get finished as quickly as I can—not to see how much I can learn.

I've stopped comparing myself to others. There will always be kids who are smarter, more athletic, better looking, taller, not as clumsy, and more organized than I am.

I know I could spend more time studying and be smarter, and I could work a little harder and be a better soccer player, and I'm going to do all those things.

I'm going to compare myself to how I was last week. If I can do math better than I could last week and I can play soccer better than I could last week, that's what matters.

The Takeaway

Comparing yourself to others is a losing endeavor. When you do that, you're always going to be disappointed. There will always be someone better than you at everything. Comparing yourself with your previous self is all that matters.

Try This

The next time you compare yourself to someone else, stop and ask yourself if you're better than you were last week. That's all that matters. If you don't think you have made any progress, then work harder and make it happen. Then be happy with yourself.

Chapter 12

Making a Speech

"Of all the liars in the world, sometimes the worst are your own fears," said famous poet Rudyard Kipling.

Like the girl pictured at the beginning of this chapter, when I got up to make my first speech, I was standing there and I couldn't remember a thing I had planned to say.

I was so scared standing in front of the class to make my speech that I was afraid I was going to pee in my pants.

I could tell myself that I wasn't in any real danger, and nothing could happen to me like it could on a bicycle or a zip line, but my body had a mind of its own and it wasn't listening to me.

I remember the time I made my first speech. I froze. My heart was racing. I couldn't think of what I had planned to say.

In this situation, my only option was to just do it, regardless of how scared and nervous I was. I wanted to run out of the room, but that wasn't an option.

Remember, standing up and making a speech is probably the scariest thing you'll ever have to do. But if you relax and realize the audience is on your side, it will help a lot.

The definition of confidence. Confidence is trusting that you can handle anything the world throws at you. It's that simple.

Say to yourself, *I can do this.* Then fake having confidence and it will look like you have confidence.

Pretend you have confidence when you need to. (Maybe saying "pretend" sounds better than saying you're going to "fake" having confidence, but I like to tell it like it is and I fake having confidence when I need to.)

Accept the fact that you will not give a perfect speech. You're almost sure to make a mistake (maybe several mistakes) when giving your speech. And when you accept this, it will take a lot of pressure off you. You'll immediately feel more relaxed.

Who knows, giving your speech might be enjoyable.

Some phrases you can say to recover when you make a mistake giving a speech

- I sure screwed that up. Let me try again.

- That wasn't what I was going to say.

- That didn't come out right.

- I forgot what I was going to say, but it would probably have been boring anyway. So, let me tell you what little I remember about what I was going to say.

These statements will get a brief chuckle from the audience, allowing you a little breather. Use that time to take a deep breath or two, and then you can continue with your speech. When you realize the audience is on your side and rooting for you, it will take a lot of pressure off you and help you relax.

Honesty plays a huge role in everything you do in life. Always be honest with yourself, with your friends, and with everybody you come in contact with. When you mess us, just say so. It's not the end of the world. People will like you better when you're honest.

The Takeaway

You gain confidence by doing things you don't know how to do or things you're not good at. If you look and act confident, people will think you are.

And if you tell your brain you're confident, it will think you are, and you will start acting confident. If you fake being confident, you'll soon feel confident. Maybe that's where the popular saying, "Fake it until you make it," came from. It's an old saying, but it works.

Try This

When you're feeling nervous about standing in front of the class, or doing anything that makes you feel uneasy, you're probably worried that you're going to make a mistake. Don't worry about the possibility that you might make a mistake. Accept the fact that you will, for sure, make a mistake, and probably more than one. So what?

When you accept that you're going to make a mistake, the fear is no longer hanging over you—at least, not as much as it was. What a relief.

The only thing the audience will remember is how you recovered. Do a good job of recovering after you make a mistake and you'll be a hero.

Chapter 13

Dealing with Emotions

> "It's not what happens to us but our response to what happens to us that hurts us."

Emotions play a big part in my life. In many situations, emotions have taken control of my life and my actions, but I've found some ways to deal with my emotions and put myself back in control.

The following chapters are about what I've learned while dealing with different emotions.

Some stories are funny, some are about embarrassing situations, and some are scary (at least, they were at the time), but they all describe how I felt and what I did while dealing with emotional situations.

As you'll learn in the following chapters, I didn't always handle things in the best way. Maybe that's a major understatement, but at other times I was a genius.

The good news is that you can learn from both my successes and my failures.

Here are the 5 emotions I've had trouble dealing with

1. Anger

2. Embarrassment

3. Sadness

4. Stress and Frustration

5. Fear

In the following chapters, I'll tell you how I have dealt with each of these different emotions. Sometimes it's not easy, but I've found that dealing with emotions is something I have to do. I guess it's part of growing up.

Of all the different emotions I deal with, I've found that anger is the most destructive, embarrassment is the most humiliating, and sadness is the emotion that can have the most lasting effect.

I sometimes wish emotions didn't exist. But then I think about how boring life would be if we felt no emotions. Without emotion, you could never feel happiness.

I'll tell you how I've handled these and other emotions in the following chapters.

Emotions are feelings and they may seem earth-shattering. But realize that these feelings won't last forever.

The Takeaway

Emotions are neither good nor bad. They're just indications that something important is happening in your life that deserves your attention.

Don't pretend you don't have feelings. It's normal to feel emotions. Imagine how boring life would be if you didn't feel any emotions.

Paying attention to your emotions will guide you towards better decisions.

I've found that my confidence grows the more I experience setbacks and deal with my emotions. I tell myself, "I can handle this."

Try This

The next time you're feeling any emotion, stop and realize that it's not the end of the world—it's just how you're feeling at the moment. Even good feelings like joy won't last forever, unfortunately.

The next time you feel a powerful emotion, don't ignore it. Pay attention to it and ask yourself, "What is this emotion trying to tell me?" When you understand that, you can then decide what to do about it.

Chapter 14

I No Longer Get Angry

> *"For every minute you're angry, you lose sixty seconds of happiness,"* said famous author Ralph Waldo Emerson.

Getting angry, mad, or upset are all ways of describing the same thing.

When someone criticized me or put me down, or when things didn't go my way, it used to set me off and I would immediately get angry.

Sometimes it wasn't a person who made me angry. I also used to get angry or frustrated at situations such as rain canceling a soccer game or the power going out while I was watching my favorite TV program.

Sometimes I got mad or angry at myself. I remember one time when my friend, Adam, and I were going fishing. I was trying to get my fishing line untangled and it was getting more tangled the longer I worked with it.

I was mad and I was angry. I don't know who I was angry at. Maybe myself. I was angry at the situation and the entire world—maybe the whole universe.

Adam laughed, but I didn't think it was funny.

When these things happened, it was like lighting a fuse on a firecracker. I would explode. Sometimes it didn't immediately show on the outside, but I got angry on the inside and I would explode later.

Emotions play a big part in our lives. Fear helps keep us safe, but it can sometimes hold us back too much and keep us from trying new things.

Anger is a different story. Anger is a destructive emotion. It clouds our judgment and gives control to the person who provoked you.

I've found that when I can eliminate anger from my life, I feel a lot happier—and I've found that I really can eliminate most of the anger in my life.

There are a few situations where anger can be useful, but not many. Sometimes anger can motivate you to do something about a problem. But even then, it's important to always keep your anger under control. Never let anger control you.

What if I told you that you could become untouchable?

No words, events, or situations could upset you, make you angry, or even bother you ever again? Wouldn't that be wonderful? I've made it happen.

My three ways I anger-proof myself

#1. Ignore insults. I don't pay attention to insults whether they are said in person or on social media. Insults only hurt me if I allow them to hurt me. If someone insults me, I stop and think, *This is their problem, not mine. It has nothing to do with me.* When I do this, the anger quickly disappears.

#2. I control what I can and ignore what I can't. Other people's words and actions are out of my control, but my reactions to their words and actions are completely within my control. The next time someone upsets you, ask yourself, "Is this within my control?" If it's not, let it go.

#3. Respond with indifference. Nothing frustrates an angry person more than someone who refuses to react. When someone tries to provoke me and I respond with calm indifference, their power over me disappears.

Here's something to consider. Famous actor Dick Van Dyke recently turned 100 years old. In an interview, when asked how he lived to be 100, he said, "Maybe it's because I never get angry." I don't know whether not getting angry helped him live to be 100 or not, but it's something to think about.

The Takeaway

You can't control what happens in your day, but you can control how you act and feel. Anger is a destructive emotion, but you have the power to anger-proof yourself. Remember that no one has the power to make you angry unless you give them that power.

Try This

The next time you feel yourself starting to get angry, remember and apply the three techniques described in this chapter.

The three anger-preventing techniques are: ignore insults, control what you can while ignoring what you can't, and respond with indifference. Do these three things and the feeling of anger will disappear almost immediately.

Another thing you can do when you start to feel angry is to stop and ask yourself, *Will this make any difference tomorrow or a week from now?* (Probably not.) If it won't matter a week from now, don't let it bother you now.

Chapter 15

Embarrassing Things Happen

> *"The best gift you can give yourself is getting over the fear of embarrassment because then you're completely free to try anything."*

Embarrassment is probably the most dreaded emotion of all. But it can be short-lived and can be the easiest to deal with.

The easiest way to deal with embarrassment is to realize that you provided enjoyment and entertainment for other people for a moment.

I'm always embarrassing myself. For example, yesterday I tripped walking up the steps at school. My books went flying everywhere and I wanted to hide, but there was no place to hide. Everyone was laughing at me.

I stood up, laughed at myself, and said, "Now for my next act." Then everyone was laughing with me instead of at me.

Keep in mind that people will remember how you recovered from an embarrassing situation more than they will remember the embarrassing thing you did.

And one other thing: remember that whatever you did to embarrass yourself, you will most likely find it funny a week later when you tell it.

When embarrassing things happen to other kids, they're funny, but when something embarrassing happens to me, it doesn't seem so funny—at least not at the moment.

Many embarrassing events are things you can laugh about later, but they're not funny when they're happening.

And, as always, embarrassing events are always funnier when they're happening to somebody else.

I found a way not to be embarrassed by things that used to terrorize me.

I've found that when I do something that makes me feel embarrassed and makes me feel like I wish I could crawl under a rock, I use one of the following statements and it makes the situation more of a funny event rather than an embarrassing situation.

Here are a few one-liners I use after an embarrassing moment

- Would you like to see my next act?

- I practiced that all week.

- You usually have to pay to see something that funny.

- I usually charge when I put on a show like that.

I found by accident that when I trip and fall, spill spaghetti sauce down the front of my shirt, or do some other embarrassing thing, I can say one of the above one-liners and more people will laugh at my comment than laugh at the embarrassing thing I did.

I discovered that these one-line comments work one time when I tripped and fell. I was so embarrassed. Without thinking, when I got up, I blurted out, "Would you like to see my next act?" Everyone laughed more at my comment than they did when I fell.

Since then, I've come up with several one-liners and I've been using these every time I do something embarrassing or stupid and they work like magic.

The cool thing is that after I come out with one of these statements or questions, the kids are laughing with me and not at me. They see me as the funny kid and not the stupid or clumsy kid.

Always remember that when embarrassing things happen to you, it's not the end of the world. It's a moment in time that most kids won't even remember a day or two later.

And anytime someone remembers what you did, they will see it as a funny event and not as something embarrassing.

The Takeaway

Every time something embarrassing happens to you (and there will be plenty of these times unless you spend your time hiding under a rock somewhere) consider it as just another funny event that you can laugh at later.

Whether you forget what you were going to say in a speech, trip and fall going up steps, or arrive at school wearing one brown shoe and one tennis shoe, your life won't be over. And the other kids won't be laughing at you for weeks or months to come like you imagine they will. They probably won't even remember the situation tomorrow.

Try This

The next time you do something that causes you to feel embarrassed, look at it as a funny event that you and the other kids can enjoy again later—that is, if anyone remembers it later. They probably won't.

Since an embarrassing event won't matter a week from now, why let it bother you now? Stop feeling embarrassed, enjoy the moment, and get on with your life.

Chapter 16

Sadness Lingers

> *"Sadness flies away on the wings of time."*

Of all the emotions, sadness is the one that can linger the longest and be the most devastating. The feelings you experience with the other emotions can be short-lived, but the effects of sadness can linger for weeks or even months.

This summer my dog, Perro, got hit by a car. I found him beside the road and he wasn't moving. We rushed him to an animal hospital and the vet told us he didn't look like he was going to make it.

The vet gave him a shot for the pain he was sure he was experiencing. Perro was in terrible shape. He was alive, but he was mostly out of it. His eyes were open, but he didn't respond when I called his name.

The vet kept him for three days and then he said, surprisingly, "Perro is doing a lot better and you can take him home."

It took over a month for Perro to get more or less back to normal, but now he seems to be as good as new.

The day I found him beside the road was one of the saddest days of my life. If Perro had died, I'm not sure how I would have handled it. I know I would have cried for a long time, but thankfully, he lived.

Dealing with sadness is way worse than embarrassment

Accept the fact that you probably can't change or do anything about what happened that made you sad. You didn't cause it and you can't fix it. But you have to go on with your life and deal with it.

There can be different degrees of sadness. And some situations may be more of a disappointment than a feeling of sadness.

For example, you could feel disappointed for a short time about making a low score on a test or about losing a soccer game, but I wouldn't call that sadness. But you could feel sad for a long time about a pet getting hurt or dying.

The two best ways to deal with sadness

#1. Talk to someone you trust—talk to your best friend, your parents, or a teacher. It's important to tell them how you feel. Don't gloss over your feelings and say that you're fine. But when you're talking to someone, also talk about some good things.

#2. Your attitude is important—it helps if you can have the attitude that you can handle whatever life throws at you. Realize that, as sad as you're feeling, it's not the end of the world. You'll feel better with time. Think about cheerful things and don't dwell on the thing or event that's making you sad. Thinking about cheerful things won't change things, and it won't make your sadness go away, but it will help make you feel less sad.

The Takeaway

Sad things are going to happen in your life. Usually, there is nothing you can do to change or fix what happened. All you can do is accept it and deal with the situation, and that's not always easy.

Try This

The next time you're feeling sad, talk to someone you trust about the situation. Talk to your best friend, your parents, your grandpa, or an uncle or aunt. It's important to tell them how you feel. When you're talking, it helps to also talk about some good and happy things as well.

Chapter 17

Stress and Frustration

> *"Relax. No one else knows what they're doing either."*

Occasionally, I feel stressed or frustrated. I sometimes get frustrated with myself and sometimes I'm frustrated with someone else or a situation. The results are the same. I can't concentrate on anything else.

I don't know if stress and frustration are the same thing or not, but at times those two words describe how I feel.

Yesterday morning, I was feeling stressed out. We had a big history test coming up. I had studied a fair amount, but obviously not enough to keep me from feeling nervous, stressed out, and frustrated with myself for not studying more.

I knew I had studied enough that I wouldn't fail the test, but I wasn't sure if I was going to do really well or just okay.

I have these feelings sometimes. I don't know what causes them, but I've found some ways to deal with my stress and frustration.

Three ways I deal with stress and frustration

Using one or more of the techniques (or tools, as I call them) that I've described below always helps me feel less frustrated and less stressed. Many times when I use these tools and techniques, my stress and frustration completely disappear—but even when they don't totally go away, doing these things usually helps a lot.

1. **Deep breathing**—I usually do this at the first sign of stress or frustration. Here's how I do it. I start by slowly breathing in through my nose for three seconds. Then I hold it for three seconds, and finally, I slowly breathe out through my mouth for three seconds. Then I continue doing this several times until I feel more relaxed. I use this technique a lot because I can do it anywhere and at any time.

I can even do it in the middle of a test or before I run out on the soccer field.

2. **A stress ball**—My grandpa taught me this trick. He gave me a foam ball that's about two inches in diameter. He called it a stress ball. It's easy to use. I squeeze it tightly and then slowly release it. Doing this helps calm me down by giving my hand something to do, and by doing it over and over it helps take my mind off of what's making me feel stressed. I keep my stress ball in my backpack so I have it handy any time I need it. (Note, you can get a foam stress ball at Walmart or order one from Amazon.)

3. **Exercise and stretching**—When I go running or do any type of hard physical activity, this always helps make my stress go away, but I can't always do exercises. I don't think it would work if I got up and ran around the room in the middle of a test. But I can always do some stretches, such as tilting my head toward each shoulder and holding it for a few seconds. I can also roll my shoulders forward and backward a few times. Doing this doesn't work as well as doing some type of strenuous exercise, but it helps some.

The Takeaway

Stress and frustration are part of life. Expect these feelings from time to time and realize that they no longer control you because now you know techniques to help get rid of these feelings.

Try This

The next time you start to feel stress or frustration, use some or all of the three techniques described in this chapter and you'll be amazed by how well they work.

Chapter 18

Fear

> *"Thinking will not overcome fear, but action will."*

Fear is one of the most valuable and useful emotions.

Without fear, there's no telling what we might do, or at least try to do. For sure, we would put ourselves in a lot of dangerous situations.

But fear can be a bad thing too—especially when it's not real. You might feel fear when you're about to make a speech in front of the class or when you get called into the principal's office (I know; I've felt fear in both situations).

Those are times when you wish you didn't feel fear. There's nothing that's going to happen to you. You won't fall through a trapdoor in the principal's office floor and disappear forever. You know that, but you feel scared just the same.

You're not really afraid, but your body is sure acting like it's afraid. Maybe it's an imaginary fear, but that can be some of the worst kinds of fear. I've experienced that fear and I know how it feels.

Fear makes us uncomfortable, and I hate the feeling, but fear helps keep us safe.

Some kids like to ride roller coasters and watch horror movies, but not me. I don't like feeling scared. I would be perfectly happy if I never felt fear again, but I'm sure that's wishful thinking.

There's a phrase made popular to keep teenagers from trying drugs when another person offers them the drugs. The phrase is "Just say no."

I use the same phrase every time other kids try to talk me into doing something I'm afraid of, like riding a roller coaster. I know that there's probably no real danger, but if I don't enjoy it, why should I do it?

Learn to say No.

There are a few situations where you need to be brave, face your fears and just do it and overcome your fear, such as standing on the bottom of the swimming pool and putting your face in the water when you're learning to swim. There's no real danger, but your body is fearful just the same.

I love to swim, but I remember how scared I was the first time I put my face in the water.

If you don't face your fears sometimes and do some things anyway, you'll miss out on a lot of fun adventures.

Sometimes you need to be brave, face your fears and do it anyway, and other times you need to listen to your fears and not do what you're afraid of.

Learning how to tell the difference and deal with each situation is part of growing up.

The Takeaway

Fear is an important and useful emotion. It helps keep us safe. But it can sometimes overpower us when it shouldn't. We have to learn how to understand when fear is real and when it's imaginary.

Try This

The next time you are feeling fearful, stop and ask yourself, *Is this something I should be fearful of or not?* Then act accordingly. That's easier said than done sometimes. If it's something you should be fearful of, follow your instincts and avoid the situation if possible.

If it's an imaginary fear, stop, take deep, slow breaths, and tell yourself that it's not an actual fear. Hopefully, your mind will listen to you and you won't feel as fearful in the situation.

Chapter 19

Finding Your Tribe

> *"The reason life works at all is that not everyone in my tribe is nuts on the same day."*

Before we moved to Panama, I had my tribe that I would hang out with a lot. And when we moved to Panama, I quickly became part of a new tribe.

The kids in Panama were friendly and I was different. I was the only kid who wasn't from Panama. A lot of kids wanted to hang out with me and talk to me.

But when we came back to the US, it took me a few weeks to become part of a tribe. The kids in the US didn't seem to be as friendly as the kids I knew in Panama.

Maybe it was just me. I felt awkward and I think I was trying too hard to fit in.

Whatever the reason, I didn't feel like I was part of a tribe for several weeks.

Lily was probably my best friend. We played together and talked. I think my tribe kind of grew from there. Adam liked to go fishing with us, so he hung out with us a lot.

What I discovered is that rather than trying hard to find a tribe that you fit in with, you should just relax, and don't sweat it. Start with one or two friends you enjoy hanging out with and let your tribe gradually grow from there.

Here are some ways to help you find your tribe

- Get involved in activities you love and enjoy.

- Start conversations with other kids you like to be around.

- When talking to another kid, listen and ask them a question about what they said. This shows that you were listening and that you're interested in what they had to say.

- Don't talk about yourself unless someone asks you

a question.

- Be your authentic self. Don't change who you are to fit in.

- Don't be overly critical. Keep in mind that no one is perfect and real kids, not perfect ones, form tribes.

- Hang out where you're likely to find the kids you would enjoy having as part of your tribe. If you like to run, fish, or play baseball, you're not likely to find many kids who like to do these things in the library.

- Spend time walking your dog. I've found that to be a great way to meet kids I like to hang out and play with.

Trying too hard to find your tribe can be frustrating. If you have only one good friend, that's fine. More will come along in due time.

The Takeaway

Finding your tribe is just something that happens. You can't force it to happen. The best way to help make it happen is to just be yourself. Don't change who you are to fit in. Sometimes you can fit in with an existing group and sometimes you build your tribe one member at a time. Kids you like to hang out with will make up your tribe.

Try This

If you haven't found your tribe yet, don't keep looking in the same places where you've been looking.

Try looking in places where kids who are interested in the same things you're interested in hang out.

Don't try too hard. Be yourself, be happy, don't be negative, don't complain, show genuine interest in other kids, and above all, listen to them. Let them talk and you'll fit in.

Chapter 20

Lily Surprised Me

> *"A single rose can be my garden. A single friend, my world."*

Lily isn't like I expected and isn't a sissy. She is more of what some people would call a tomboy. She is energetic and independent and likes to go fishing, play in the creek and do things outside.

Lily and I spent a lot of time playing together this past summer before school started.

But after school started, we were both busy and didn't have as much time to play. Also, the weather hasn't always been as good for playing outside as it was all summer, but we have been able to play some lately.

Lily doesn't have a brother or sister, so she doesn't have any kids at home to talk to. Maybe that's why she's always talking to me and asking me so many questions. She thinks I know everything.

She asked me how I liked living in Panama and whether I enjoy playing soccer. She asked me which teachers I like best, and the list goes on and on.

These are all questions that are easy to answer.

She has asked my advice and valued my opinion on a lot of things. Maybe that's why I enjoy spending so much time with her.

That's how I realized that if you want someone to want to be your friend and spend time with you, ask them for advice and ask them what they think about things. This shows them you respect and value their opinions.

When you do this, they will immediately like you. It's easy to like kids who value your opinions. That's one of the many things that I learned by spending time with Lily.

Lily and I went fishing again last Saturday. She loves to go fishing. This time we caught some fish. Not big ones, but big enough that they put up a fight. Lily really enjoyed that.

My little brother, Noah, went fishing with us. He had fun too. He caught his first fish.

Lily is a year younger than I am. I think most kids like to have friends who are their own age. I usually do too, but having a friend who is a little younger than I am has worked out just fine.

In fact, it has been better than fine. We have a lot of fun and I'm enjoying being friends with Lily.

I've found that younger friends look at life a little differently and they are interested in different things. That makes my life more interesting. Kids from different backgrounds and different nationalities are interesting as well.

After spending time with my dog, Perro, Lily decided she wanted a dog. Her parents got her a puppy for her birthday. I had never been around a puppy before. Perro was already a grown dog when we got him from the pound.

Just like younger people are different and interesting, a younger dog is way different from an older dog.

Lily's little puppy is jet black and she named him Snowball. She has a sense of humor and laughs a lot. She's happy most of the time, and she doesn't complain about many things. Sometimes things bother her, but not often.

She likes to go bike riding, fly a kite, and do things outside, like Billy and I used to do, but she also likes to play board games such as Monopoly. We've been doing both things a lot.

I miss having Billy around to play with like we did when he lived across the street where Lily lives now, but I'm having fun with Lily when we have time to play. I'm looking forward to this summer when we can be outside more and have more time to play without having to go to school.

Lily has a journal and she writes in it every day. When she does that, she calls it journaling. It's not the same as writing in a diary.

Writing is not something I like to do, but she loves doing it. I think she just writes what she did that day, what happened, or what she was thinking. She writes a little every day. She calls that enjoyable. Not me. I love math, but I hate to write.

She doesn't have any trouble when a teacher assigns writing a paper as homework, but I dread having to write a paper.

The Takeaway

Having a friend who is different from me makes life more enjoyable. It's good to have friends who share your interests, but having friends who are younger, have different backgrounds, or different nationalities can be interesting and enjoyable as well.

Try This

Consider becoming friends with someone who is younger than you are or different from you in some way. Younger kids love it when an older kid pays attention to them. I think you'll find that spending time with a younger kid, or someone different from you, will be a lot more fun than you imagined.

Chapter 21

Bad Things Happen

"I've lived through some terrible things in my life, some of which actually happened," said famous author Mark Twain.

Every time I turn around, something else bad happens in my life.

Many of the bad things that happen in my life are things I can't do anything about. They're out of my control. All I can do is complain, so that's what I do.

I mostly complain to myself because when I complain to grown-ups, they all tell me the same thing. They just give me a lecture and tell me to be patient and things will get better.

How long do I have to be patient for things to get better?

I've been patient for what seems like forever and nothing has gotten any better. I think most of my problems have gotten worse.

I was moping around last Saturday when my grandpa had stopped by. He stops by a lot and I enjoy talking to him. He listens to me and doesn't lecture me.

He asked me what was wrong and I said, "Nothing."

He said, "You can do better than that."

Then I told him about my problems and all the things that were going wrong in my life.

He said, "So what are you doing about your problems?"

I said, "What am I doing? There's nothing I can do except complain and be patient and wait for things to change."

Grandpa didn't give me a lecture and tell me what I should do. He just said, "How is complaining and waiting for things to change working for you?"

Here are some of my problems

- I didn't make the starting lineup for the soccer team.

- My friend Billy moved away and no longer lives across the street.

- They moved me to a harder math class. They call it an advanced class, but what it really means is that there's more homework that I have to do and it's not easy like the class I was in.

Over the weekend, I decided that, good, bad, or indifferent, I was going to do something about my problems. Being patient and complaining weren't working.

Here's what I decided to do

For soccer: I probably didn't make the starting lineup for the soccer team because I had not tried hard enough. That was true. I had not been trying very hard. I just enjoyed playing and hanging out with the kids on the team. Starting Monday, I was going to put a lot more effort into playing and really making a difference. And I was going to start running to build up my stamina.

Missing Billy: I think it was how I was looking at things. After all, Lily had moved into the house where Billy used to live and she is a lot more fun to play with. She's almost always happy and she doesn't complain often. And I've been talking with Billy on my computer using a free app called Zoom that allows us to see each other on the computer screen. That's almost as good as seeing him in person, and in some ways even better.

The harder math class: If I stop complaining and look at the facts, there are some good things about the advanced math class. All the kids in that class really like math and the teacher enjoys math, so she makes the class more fun.

Before you decide you can't do anything about a problem, look at it again differently and see if you can't find a way to make things better.

There's an old saying: *"Where there's a will, there's a way."* It's not always true, but it's probably true more times than you realize.

The Takeaway

I've found that, when I have problems, waiting for things to get better doesn't work and complaining doesn't help. I have to make changes in my life to fix things and I have to realize that there are some things I have no control over, and there's nothing I can do to change those things, but I can change more things than I used to think I could. Best of all, I can change my attitude toward things. Most of the time, that helps a lot.

Try This

Write down the three biggest problems in your life right now. Look at each one and decide if they're things you can control.

Look hard, and with an open mind, and see if you can't think of something you can do to fix the problem or at least make it less of a problem.

I've found that when I write down what I'm going to do, I'm a lot more likely to take action and do something about the problem.

And if you find something you can't fix, such as rain canceling today's field trip, understand that it won't ruin your world. Accept it and move on with your life. I've fount that when I change my attitude, that fixes a lot of problems.

Chapter 22

Dealing with Peer Pressure

"Peer pressure is just that—pressure."

Peer pressure is when you feel pushed, encouraged, or pressured to do something you don't feel comfortable doing or don't want to do.

Your peers are the people you hang out with, but they may or may not be your friends. At least you may find out that they are not your true friends.

Whether it's something you think might be dangerous, not the right thing to do, or you're being pressured to go along with the crowd so you'll fit in, don't fall for peer pressure. You're in charge of yourself.

Last week, I was on the playground and a few of the older kids were over in the corner of the playground, out of sight of the teachers, smoking a cigarette one kid had brought from home. They wanted me to try it.

It wasn't something I wanted to do. I didn't like the smell of it and I knew some of the health risks associated with it. My uncle had smoked and he died of lung cancer.

Several of the other kids were doing it, but smoking a cigarette, even taking one puff, was something I didn't want to do.

Even if you would like to fit in, and it's something more or less harmless, such as kids trying to convince you to get on a roller coaster at the fair, if you don't want to, you can say no.

Self-imposed peer pressure

Don't fall victim to self-imposed peer pressure either. What this means is that you put pressure on yourself to do something so you'll fit in. You will always feel tempted to do what others do to be accepted and fit in.

But don't do anything you don't want to do just because everyone else is doing it.

Other kids will respect you more, and you'll feel better about yourself if you stick to your convictions than you will if you give in to doing something you don't want to do.

The kids kept pushing me to take one puff of the cigarette. They said, "You'll like it."

That's when I said, "When I say no, I mean no. Is that too hard for you to understand?" Maybe I should have been more polite, but I was tired of them hounding me to do something I didn't want to do.

I felt good about myself after I had stood my ground, and it worked. They didn't ask or pressure me again.

Remember that you have the right to say no. When other kids find out that peer pressure doesn't work on you, they'll respect you a lot more.

If you notice that certain of your friends are always pushing you to do things you don't want to do, or trying to make you feel bad for saying no, maybe it's time to rethink those friendships.

Surround yourself with friends who respect your choices. True friends won't pressure you to do things you feel uncomfortable with.

The Takeaway

You will always have to deal with peer pressure, but more so as a kid. Learn to say no and hold your ground. Realize that the kids trying to get you to do something that's not in your best interest are not your true friends.

They're not looking out for your best interests. These kids may be kids you hang out with, but when they're pressuring you to do something you don't want to do, or that's not in your best interest, that tells you they're not your loyal friends.

Try This

Learn to say "No" and stick to it. Be on the lookout for situations where kids are using peer pressure to get you to do something you don't want to do. Be ready to say no and stick to it. You'll feel much better about yourself. Remember that it's your life and you have the right to say no.

Chapter 23

The Power of "Yet"

> *"'I can't do that' ends the story. 'I can't do that yet' means anything is possible."*

I love spending time with my grandpa. He taught me a lot about the power of "yet."

I'm always talking to myself—sometimes out loud and sometimes just in my head.

I say things to myself that I wouldn't dare say to a friend.

For example, when I make a poor grade on a science test, I'll say to myself, "You're no good at science." When I miss a shot in a soccer game, I'll say to myself, "You're terrible at playing soccer and you'll never be any good."

My brain hears these words and believes every word I tell it. These words sound so final and like there's nothing I can do about the situation.

But when I add the word "yet," that changes everything and opens up possibilities. With possibilities such as a little more time spent studying science or a little more effort put into playing soccer, I will get better. That's a much better message to send to my brain.

When I tell myself that I'm not good at science or soccer **yet**—that gives my brain a whole different message. All I need is more time studying science, and more time practicing soccer, and I'll be good at both.

Where I am now is not where I'll always be.

The next time you catch yourself thinking negative thoughts—such as, *I'll never be able to sing or play a musical instrument in front of a class*—stop and say, "I haven't done this **yet**, but I know that with some practice and studying, I'm sure I can do it."

When I'm trying to learn something new, I'm sure I will do poorly in the beginning. I don't focus on what I can't control. I focus on what I can control.

I can control how much I practice and how much I study. I can't control the outcome, but I can control these two things.

My grandpa told me that when you're learning a new skill, you shouldn't compare yourself to others. There will always be somebody better at it than you are. Instead, compare yourself with how you did last week. You'll never be perfect, but your goal should be to strive to be better than you were last week.

He also said not to compare yourself with how you did yesterday. You'll have good and bad days and you shouldn't expect to see noticeable improvements in one day—at least, not every day.

I've learned to love my mistakes

Failing and making mistakes is the only way you learn. What if you had decided that you would not get in the pool until you learned how to swim or you would not get on a bicycle until you learned how to ride it?

You tried those two things knowing you were going to make mistakes. The good thing is that after making mistakes, you learned to swim and to ride a bicycle.

Look at other challenges in your life with the same determination. Learn to love your mistakes. That's how you learn new skills and gain confidence.

I've found that I gain confidence by trying things and making mistakes.

The Takeaway

Don't be afraid of making mistakes. Accept that making mistakes is normal and that it can be a good thing. The more mistakes I make means the more new things I'm trying, so the more mistakes I make, the more things I'm learning.

Try This

Every time you think you can't do something, don't say that you can't do it. Instead, say (or think), "I can't do this **yet**." Adding the word yet gives your brain a completely different message and opens up a world of possibilities.

Chapter 24

Final Thoughts

> *"Congratulations. You made it to the end of the book."*

You've learned a lot of skills from your **Kids' Secret Playbook of Life**.

Better days for you are ahead. Not all of your days will be perfect. That doesn't happen to anybody. Your days will be better because you now know how to deal with just about anything the world throws at you.

The skills you've learned are not only skills to help you survive and enjoy school, but these skills will also be useful for the challenges you'll face in everyday life as you continue growing up.

You're the hero in your own story.

You've made it from zero to hero. You're off on your adventure of life. Using what you have learned from this book, you're ready for a happy, adventurous life.

One thing's for sure. Your life will not be boring.

Look forward to all the joys and challenges you'll face along the way.

Remember that every problem has a solution and mistakes are not failures because every mistake is a lesson that you learn something from.

You're stronger and smarter after every mistake.

You're still growing up. You don't have all the answers. Even adults don't have all the answers. Some days you'll feel you have everything figured out and some days you won't know which way to turn. That's normal.

I know this book didn't solve all your problems. That would be impossible.

I don't even know all the problems you're having. I haven't even solved all of my own problems.

Even though I've discussed several problems and situations in this book, I'm sure I haven't experienced all the things that could happen to me or to you.

These techniques haven't solved all my problems. I keep having additional problems every day.

I think life would be kind of boring if everything went exactly as expected all the time. But I think there are some days when I would for sure like to have fewer problems.

Maybe the way I learned and dealt with being a kid and solving my problems was not always the best way to handle things, but I'm still alive and life is still going on.

As I get older, I'll probably find better ways to deal with some things that have happened to me so far.

For most problems, there's no one perfect solution or answer.

As I've learned from my older sister, there will be bad hair days and there will be rainy days, but the sun will always shine again soon.

Some last thoughts

Keep reading books, learning, experiencing life, and enjoying one day at a time. That's what I'm doing and I'm loving my life.

Don't believe everything you read. Question what you read. If something sounds too good to be true, it probably is.

Be especially careful about believing what you see on social media. Also, be careful about who you become "friends" with on social media, and about what you tell them about yourself.

The Takeaway

Life is not a destination, so never say, "I'll be happy when . . ."

Life is a journey, so enjoy the journey and look forward to what happens next in your life.

Being a kid is fun, but growing up can be fun too. Look forward to each new day.

Try This

Whether you're a little kid or a big kid, keep an open mind, don't be negative, and always remember that all problems have a solution.

Be happy and try to make as many other people happy as you can while you're on your journey.

Chapter 25

Did You Like This Book?

> *"If you liked this book and found it helpful, I need your help."*

Amazon values reviews and the number of reviews that readers post on Amazon has a lot to do with how high Amazon ranks a book in their search results.

And of course, the higher a book ranks the better it sells. I would love it if you would take a minute and post an honest review on Amazon. You really can do it in a minute or less.

I read and appreciate every review.

You may need to get your parents to help you post the review on Amazon because the review has to be posted by the person who actually bought the book.

Here's the easy way to post a review

Search Amazon for the title of the book, *Kids' Secret Playbook of Life*, and it will take you to the book's detail page on Amazon.

Scroll about halfway down the page until you see the yellow bar graph on the left side. Then click on the box below the graph that says,

"Write a customer review." (It's the box the arrow is pointing to in the following screenshot.)

Next, click on the number of stars (five is a good number) and then go to the box that says, **"Add a written review,"** and write one or two sentences. Then go up to where it says, **"Add a headline,"** and add a headline, click on **"Submit,"** and you're all finished. It's that simple.

Posting your review will take you less than a minute and it will mean the world to me. It's not a review of the entire book. It's a comment on one thing you liked about the book. What you say is not so important—because few people read the reviews anyway—but everybody looks at the total number of reviews, so the important thing is to post one.

The main takeaway from this chapter:

If you post a review, I'll be eternally grateful—or at least I'll be grateful for a long, long time.

Your friend,

Panama Pete

P.S. Note: I didn't use AI to write any part of this book. I don't even know how to use it. Maybe I'll learn one day, but for now, AI is Greek to me.

P.P.S. If you liked this book, I'm sure you'll like my previous book, **"Confidence and Life Skills for Kids Ages 8-12."** You can find it on Amazon at the link below:

https://www.amazon.com/dp/1947020269

Made in United States
Orlando, FL
07 January 2026

76414684R00069